ARENʼT YOU LUCKY!

For Tom, Maddy and Claire

A Red Fox Book

Published by Random House Children's Books
20 Vauxhall Bridge Road, London SW1V 2SA

A division of Random House UK Ltd
London Melbourne Sydney Auckland
Johannesburg and agencies throughout the world

First published by The Bodley Head Children's Books 1990

Red Fox edition 1992
Reprinted 1993
Copyright © Catherine Anholt 1990
The right of Catherine Anholt to be identified as the author and
illustrator of this work has been asserted by her in accordance
with the Copyright, Designs and Patents Act, 1988.

ISBN 0 09 992160 X

Printed and bound in Belgium
by Proost International Book Production

Aren't you Lucky!

Catherine Anholt

RED FOX

At first it was just me on my own.

Just Mummy and Daddy and me.

I didn't have a brother then.
I'd never even thought about it.

Then one day Daddy told me,
'Mummy's going to have another baby.
Aren't we lucky!'

APRIL

MAY

JUNE

JULY

AUGUST

'The baby will take a long time to
grow inside her,' he said.
'We'll all have to be very patient.'

SEPTEMBER

OCTOBER

NOVEMBER

DECEMBER

But I got tired of waiting.

Then at last the waiting was over.

Mummy was going to the hospital to have the baby.

but I had Granny to look after me.

I didn't want her to go,

The next day we all went to visit and . . .

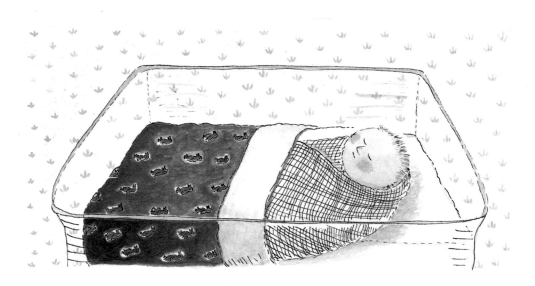

there was my little brother!

'Aren't you lucky!' said Granny.

'Do you think he looks like me or like Daddy?'
asked Mummy.
'I think he looks like a raspberry!' I said.

'Look he's waking up now.'

'He can't talk yet . . .

but he can cry alright,

especially when he's hungry.'

'Can he play with me?'

'No, he's not strong enough
to sit up on his own.'

'Hello little baby,' I said.

'I'm your sister.'

After that it was me and my brother.

Mummy and Daddy, my brother and me.

Then lots of people came to see my baby brother,

and they all said, 'Aren't you lucky!'

But sometimes I didn't feel lucky at all.

It took me a long time to get used to that baby.

I always had to wait.

He didn't know how to play.

He cried when I made music,

but no one got cross when
he made a noise.

Mummy asked me to try to be good but . . .

I didn't want my tea.

I wanted Mummy to play party with me.

I made myself all spotty.

I just wanted to be a baby too.

My brother even cried in the bath.

'Thank goodness for a little peace and quiet,'
said Daddy.

But it didn't last long!

In the end, Mummy got tired.

'If only I had someone
who could help me,' she said.

'I wish I had a big girl
who could feed my baby.'

'I could do that,' I said.

Then as the baby grew bigger,
we found lots of ways that I could help . . .

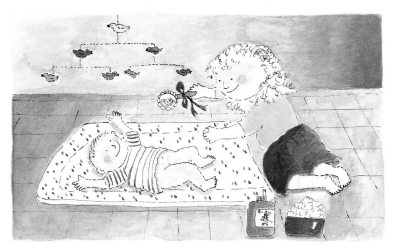

I make him laugh.

I brush his hair.

I show him my books,

and do my jazzy dance.

There were all kinds of things that we could enjoy together.

Going for a walk.

Looking at the moon.

Having a bath,

and a bedtime cuddle.

Now he likes me best of all,

and whenever people see me with my brother,
they say,

'Isn't he lucky!'